THE ALPHA BID

DISTINGUISHED GENTLEMEN SERIES

THE ALPHA BID

DISTINGUISHED GENTLEMEN SERIES

TY YOUNG

The Alpha Bid: Distinguished Gentlemen Series

Author: Ty Young

Publisher: Young Dreams Publications, Chicago, IL
www.youngdreamsbig.com

ISBN: 978-0-578-52315-6
LCCN: TBD

Influence

The one known as the *Alpha to the Highest Alpha*.

The one I call, *the one whom I love*.

Acknowledgments

During this process, I acknowledged to myself that I knew nothing about writing a romance novel. While I've had the pleasure of having a couple of great loves in my life, I acknowledge that I lived in a fairytale bubble throughout my adolescence and most of my twenties. Until one day, I'd say when I was like 33, I realized and accepted the hard-truth that that 'ish in the movies doesn't happen like that in real life.

Thus the reason we have romance writers, romantic comedies, and the greatest love stories we'd ever see on the big screen. This goes out to all the writers who know how to write a great romance.

Author's Note

When I agreed to join this wonderful group of writers for this anthology series, I must have been drunk. But I'm glad I did it. While I'm not a newbie to writing novels, I am a newbie to romance. As I wrote this quick read – it literally is a quick read – I had to continually redirect myself from where I wanted to actually take this story.

While the goal was a novella, you're getting more like a novelette – I pray that it's a good one to the readers who've invested their time into this series. I had to channel the inner Black version of the Lifetime Channel to pull out what I wanted to express about romance and love. I knew immediately that my *Distinguished Gentleman* would be an alpha male, but he's a tamed one because I recognized he had a beautiful soul who actually wanted to be in love and not just be in control.

I'm also happy because I extended myself a little writer's liberty and veered off my usual subject matter genre of what I call urban-Christian fiction. So I pray that you all enjoy this freedom with me and if I deem to be any good at it, I may dabble in it more in future works.

Contents

The Auction

"I don't know how I let Mama Peaches talk me into doing this bachelor auction," Coby said aloud to himself as he admired his impressive physique in the mirror backstage.

Coby was the first to go out on stage, and he was very nervous. While he was confident in his looks, he never thought about being auctioned off to a crowd of women before. He was so used to being the aggressor when it came to women, it was hard for him to wrap his mind around women being aggressive toward him.

He went back to his dressing station and grabbed his brush to give his smooth, shiny waves one last brush through.

The stage producer yelled out to all the men backstage, "Five minutes until go time, gentlemen!"

Coby looked at the stage producer through the reflection of the mirror and continued to brush his hair one last time. He let out a burly sigh and then smoothed his hand over his chocolatey-skinned face and full beard. He needed to give himself a pep talk, "OK! You got this, Coby!"

Coby looked at all the men around the room as they began to form a line behind the stage curtain waiting for the announcer to start the auction. Coby took his spot at the head of the line, as he was the first bachelor to make his debut. Suddenly he felt a slap on the shoulder from the bachelor behind him.

Erin, bachelor number two chuckled, "Ready to be eaten alive, man?"

Coby shook his head no, "Man, Mama Peaches is wild for this one. But she's always been a frisky old lady, so I don't even know why I'm surprised." They both burst out into laughter as the music from the stage started blaring. The high spirited music had the ladies whooping and hollering. The bachelor auctioneer suddenly emerged on the stage.

"Alright, alright, alright, ladies! Are y'all ready to see some of the most eligible bachelors in Southlake Park?"

"Wooooooohooooo!" One feisty lady screamed who was sitting in the front row.

"Bring on the sexy chocolate!" Another lady said as she held her money up high, waving it from side to side.

Ryse Taylor was sitting in the front row. She had a smirk on her face seeming somewhat nonchalant about the entire experience. One of her business colleagues had

hyped her up to do the auction as a way for her to meet

someone. She'd been striking out in the dating

department, and her friend thought this would be an

excellent way for her to meet someone as well.

"Girl, loosen up." Mehgan, Ryse's friend said as

she nudged her.

"Girl, I'm loose. I just want to get this over with. I

can't believe I'm giving away my money to win a date. It

feels desperate."

"Remember, it's for a good cause! You're helping

rebuild Southlake Park! We both grew up in this

neighborhood. We need this revitalization!" Meghan

chirped.

Ryse picked up her shot of cognac and downed it

in my gulp. She pulled her hair out of the tight, elegant

ponytail she had in and ran her fingers through her hair.

The Alpha Bid: Distinguished Gentlemen Series

She shook her hair to free herself of the stuffy energy she was holding in. "You're right! Let me let go and let God!"

The two women laughed, and Ryse caught the waitress' attention to bring her and Meghan another shot of the cognac. The waitress quickly brings over the shots, the two toasts and throws back the shots just in enough time to concentrate on the first bachelor.

"OK, ladies! We're starting this auction off right!" The auctioneer said as her voice came back into focus as the ladies prepared themselves for the auction to start. "Coming to the stage is a chocolate brother who is in charge! His magnetic energy will draw you in, and you won't be able to turn yourself loose. He is 35, president of the Urban Choice Channel, never been married, no kids, and he's ready to be in charge of you!"

The ladies in the audience went bananas when they heard Coby's stats! Some of the ladies began to fan themselves as they imagined in their minds what Coby looked like. Ryse was sitting in her seat with the same smirk on her face staring intently at the curtain waiting for the bachelor to appear on the stage.

"Ladies, welcome to the stage, Jacob St. Williams, aka Coby, aka The Alpha!!!" The auctioneer roared!

Behind the curtain, Coby blew out air when his walking music started. Coby may have been a bit young, but his soul was old. His walking music was Teddy P's "Close the Door," he could hear the women swoon as the opening chords of the legendary track began to play. Coby laughed to himself as he blushed within from hearing all the women yell, waiting for him to come from behind the curtain.

"Alright, man, gone on out there. They're waiting for you." Erin said, giving him a slight encouraging push.

Coby blew out air one more time and then pushed his hands through the curtain to walk out. He stepped out and emerged barefoot in his white linen pants and unbuttoned white linen short sleeved shirt. He was dark chocolate, and the white linen looked heavenly against his skin. All of the women melted.

Ryse was sat in her seat as she watched Coby. She wasn't sure what it was, but something about him made her lady parts flutter a bit. She was pleasantly surprised as she wasn't expecting this gorgeous man to come from behind the curtain, yet she didn't make a move. Same smirk but her eyes were looking him up and down.

Coby looked around the room at the ladies, still standing in the same spot. The auctioneer hyped Coby up to the ladies, while she drooled over him herself. The women were so mesmerized that no one had raised their paddle to make a bid yet.

Coby began to move around the stage, his glide was just as smooth as the Teddy P. track playing in the background. He prowled like a lion across the stage in a natural seductive way. He didn't even have to try it, just flowed effortlessly from his energy. As he looked across the room suddenly he locked eyes with Ryse.

The auctioneer was speaking in the background. "OK, ladies! This auction will start off at $100 let's get this party started because I know there has to be a lady that wants to take Coby home tonight!"

Coby kept his gaze on Ryse, and everyone has noticed it. He suddenly flashed his bright, white smile at her and then winked. The ladies swoon even more. Coby circled the stage once more and then locked eyes with Ryse again. For some reason, she was unable to take the unimpressed smirk off her face, which betrayed the way her body was feeling as her lady parts began to thump a bit more like a heartbeat.

Coby walked to the front of the stage right in front of where Ryse was sitting. He confidently lowered his body into a baseball catcher's stance in front of Ryse. She's drawn into him but didn't say a word or blink her eyes. Coby licked his cocoa butter soft lips and said, "You know you like this chocolate." He got up quickly and went back to working the crowd.

Ryse's lady parts made a strong pulsation. Then Ryse aggressively lifted her hand up with her paddle tightly clinched, "$100!"

The ladies screamed. Meghan looked as Ryse and started laughing hysterically and said, "That's what I'm talking about!"

That's all the other ladies needed to get the bidding war going.

"$150!" An older lady said while staring at Ryse.

Before Ryse could make her counter bid another bidder joined in, "$250," a younger, vibrant woman yelled.

Ryse looked at her sternly and yelled, "$500!" She didn't think twice about doubling the bid quickly. It caught everyone by surprise, even Coby. He quickly looked back at Ryse, breaking his attention from another lady that he had made eye contact with.

They both locked eyes again and this time Ryse let a bit of her guard down and showed Coby a toothy smile. Coby walked back over to Ryse's side of the stage, and he bends down again, "I knew you liked this chocolate," Coby said taunting Ryse. He quickly stood back up and went to work more of the stage.

"$600!" The older lady, the first counter bidder said.

Ryse gave her a playful sister girl look and raised her paddle again, "$700!" She yelled and gave her a bold look to counter the bid.

"$800!" The older lady said loud and proud!

"Wow, y'all aren't playing with Coby, I see! Don't y'all hurt each other, now. We have more bachelors to go!" The auctioneer said as she was eating up the friendly comradery.

As Coby was working the stage, it was something about Ryse that kept pulling him her way. It was clear to everyone that Ryse was the girl he wanted to win the bid. As they made goo-goo eyes at each other, Ryse looked back at the older bidder and countered again. "One-thousand!!!" Ryse said firmly, while she looked the older bidder in the eyes.

Everyone diverted their attention to the older bidder waiting to see if she was going to counter.

"Ooooohhhh, $1,000! Going once!" The auctioneer said.

Ryse folded her arms, daring the older bidder to counter.

"$1,000, going twice!" The auctioneer said anxiously.

Ryse looked at the older bidder. The older bidder then suddenly stood up, Ryse smile turns to a sudden frown as she feared the older bidder was going to counter. In a turn of events the older bidder curtseys to Ryse as she elegantly folded on the bid.

"Sold! To the powerful lady in purple!" The auctioneer said, referring to Ryse's purple, form-fitting cami-dress.

Ryse smiled, and then she and Meghan stood up and hugged each other. Ryse looked at Coby, and he saluted her before he walked off the stage.

"Chile, that was intense. I thought that old lady was going to bid you out!" Meghan said.

"Girl, me too. I don't know what else is behind that curtain, but Mr. Coby got my attention." Ryse said as she fanned herself.

Soon an auction production assistance came to Ryse's table, "Ma'am, would you like to go backstage and meet your bachelor?"

Ryse smiled, "Of course!" She grabbed her purse and waved bye to Meghan. She was a bit nervous about coming face-to-face with Coby, but no one could tell how nervous she was by her sultry strut.

As they headed toward the backstage area, Ryse could faintly hear the auctioneer introduce bachelor number two, and all the ladies yelled and screamed again as he appeared on stage.

The auction assistant lead Ryse backstage to Coby's dressing station as he was wiping the sweat from his brow. He quickly gathered himself and gave his attention toward the two ladies.

"Coby, I'd like you to meet the woman who won the date with you."

Ryse held out her hand to shake Coby's, "Ryse Taylor, a pleasure to meet you."

Coby smiled and firmly grabbed Ryse's hand, "Coby St. Williams, a pleasure to meet you as well." Coby then pulled a hesitant Ryse into his bosom and gave her a seductive hug. Ryse blushed and quickly pulled herself out of his control. The production assistant excused herself to leave the two to get better acquainted.

"So, what did I win?" Ryse asked.

"Wow, you just get right to it, huh? I like a woman that knows what she wants." Coby smiled and offered Ryse a seat in his chair at his station, she obliged.

"Well, I'm not big on small talk, and it is an auction, so I want to know what I earned for $1,000," Ryse said as she smiled and looked up at Coby.

"OK, well let's get to it. I've arranged for a private dinner at Mae & Company for the evening and a day spa event at The Luxe Spa Room. How does that sound?"

"That sounds amazing. How were you able to get private dining accommodations at Mae & Company?" Ryse asked puzzled. The expensive, celebrity-frequented restaurant usually has reservations booked out for months.

"Not to be arrogant, but did you not hear that I'm the president of The Urban Choice Channel? I can get reservations at mostly any restaurant I want."

"I guess you can. Does being the president of UCC also get you anybody you want?" Ryse bantered back.

"I guess so." Coby smiled as he picked up Ryse's hand and kissed the back of it.

They conversed for a bit longer and exchanged numbers, then Ryse excused herself back to the auction room and watched the other ladies bid for more bachelors.

The Date

"So are you ready?" Meghan asked over the phone as Ryse is stared at herself in the mirror.

"Girl, yes! I couldn't get Coby off my mind. That's unusual for me. But he made it easy. He kept sending me flowers every other day. My darn foyer looks like a funeral home." Ryse chuckled as she smoothed her hand down her tightly fitted, knee-length, black, casual cotton dress.

"I find that admirable. He's showing his interest."

Ryse placed her two-carat diamond studs in her and scrunched up her face, "Girl, admirable? He's obligated to the date. We haven't even spoken on the phone since the auction. I don't even know if he likes me like that."

Meghan huffed, "He likes you. I don't think he would have sent flowers every other day for two weeks just out of the obligation of a date."

"Well, he is a charming man. I wouldn't put anything past him. I'm going to enjoy this day and not think about much else."

"See there you go, being cynical again. That's why you don't have a man now."

"Naw, see you got it wrong. A lot of these men are stuck in the Stone Age. They forget that women can do things for themselves. I work just as hard as the next man. I don't need nobody trying to run my life." Ryse said as she slipped on her causal red flats.

"Where did all that come from?" Meghan was audibly irritated. "Please don't take that energy on this date. He's about to pick you up for a nice spa and then a wonderful dinner. Can you please try to enjoy it?"

"OK. OK. You always got to be the voice of reason. I don't know, I just think I had a flashback of dealing with Craig's crazy, controlling tale."

"Chile, something…" Meghan paused for a second as the phone fumbled in her hands.

"Hello?" Ryse said.

"Girl, my bad, I almost drop the darn phone trying to multitask with these pots making breakfast."

"Oh. OK, well let me get off this phone and finish my makeup. Coby will be due here in about ten minutes." The two ladies exchanged kissing sound into the receivers and ended the call.

Ryse wasn't a heavy makeup wearer. She decided to do light makeup for the morning. She knew they were headed straight to the spa and didn't want to do too much touching up after laying down on the massage table. She brushed her eyebrows and put a bit of concealer under her eyes. She then applied a touch of

mascara and nude lipstick. It was 8am, she felt that was

an appropriate day look for the occasion.

Suddenly as she was walked to her bedroom to

grab her purse and garment bag, her phone rang. She

looked at the caller ID to see that it was Coby calling.

Ryse smiled, "Good morning, sir."

"Well, good morning to you, too. Are you ready? I

believe I'm outside your lovely home."

"Yes, I'm ready! I was just grabbing my things."

Ryse grabbed her keys and flung her purse and garment

bag over her shoulders and headed to the front of her

home. She peeked out of the window to see what car

Coby pulled up in. She was surprised to see a town car,

for some reason she expected him to drive them himself.

Ryse opened the front door and stepped onto the

porch. She waved at the car, although she was able to see

Coby from behind the jet-black tinted windows. She turned to close and lock the door and proceeded to walk down her porch steps. The driver got out of the car and stood ready to greet Ryse as she approached the car.

He tipped his hat to her, "Good morning, Ms. Taylor," he said and then opened the back passenger door. Ryse entered the car as if she was used to that type of treatment.

"Good morning, beautiful," Coby said as Ryse settled in the car. Coby then leaned over and kissed her on the cheeks. Ryse felt her lady parts thumping again.

Ryse blushed, "Well, good morning! Not sure why I expected that you would be driving us yourself."

"Usually on a normal date I would, but this is special. No one has ever bid $1,000 to win a date with me. I figured I needed to give you your money's worth," Coby beamed.

"Well, I'm sure it will be worth it." Ryse looked forward as the driver pulled from in front of her house. "So am I dressed appropriately for the first half of our date?"

Coby gave Ryse a once-over, "Absolutely! It won't matter because you won't be in those clothes for long."

Ryse looked puzzled, "Excuse me?"

Coby laughed, "It's not what you think I mean. After breakfast, we will be relaxing with a massage and pamper session. You'll disrobe and put on the special spa clothing they have there."

"Oh…" Ryse side-eyed.

"You didn't eat breakfast yet, did you?"

"No, I didn't. Actually, I wasn't really sure what to do. You didn't give me many details about what we were actually doing. You just sent flowers for two weeks."

Coby snickered again, "I like the element of surprise. I want you to just sit back and enjoy this ride, but I get the feeling that it will be hard for you to do. You like to be in control, don't you?"

"I wouldn't say that. But I am the CEO of my own investment firm. I'm sort of used to telling people what to do," Ryse pursed her lips.

"Well, you won't be telling me what to do around here. You should learn to follow. It will be good for you."

Ryse didn't take too kindly of his previous statement and rolled her eyes. She was quiet for the next few minutes until a thought sparked up for a different conversation emerged in her mind.

"So, what's an average day like for the president of UCC like?" Ryse asked.

Coby turned to Ryse from staring out of the window, "Well, it honestly depends upon the day. Some days are full of meetings with program directors trying to see what the next big breakthrough show is going to be. Other times I'm entertaining producers at meetings. Then there are times like this where I'm enjoying life in the company of a beautiful woman."

Ryse gave Coby a nonchalant sister girl look and pursed her lips again. "Is that right? Well, how many beautiful ladies' company, besides me, are you currently enjoying?"

"Let's just say I've been on a short hiatus for about six months. My last relationship didn't go too well. We were on two different pages."

"Well, what page were you on?"

Coby shrugged, "I think I was more on relationship mode, looking to secure my queen. She wasn't quite ready for that. She had just started her career, and she was more focused on securing the bag than securing my love."

"Ouch!" Ryse cringed.

"Yeah, I know. But I'm over it now. I've been out on a few dates here and there, but nothing major. This is actually the first nice date I've been on in a while. Every other date for the past six months has been more like meetings at the coffee shop or quick brunches."

"Well, I think I should feel privileged, even though I had to pay for it." They both laughed.

They soon arrived at The Luxe Spa Room. The driver pulled into the round-about and quickly exited the vehicle to let Ryse and Coby out of the car. Coby grabbed their belongs from the driver who retrieved the items from the trunk, and they walked into the building greeted by the hostess.

"Pleasure to see you again, Mr. St. Williams! Your companion is lovely." The hostess said to Coby and bowed to Ryse.

"I see you come here often," Ryse said.

"Actually I do. I believe in taking care of myself. Massages and manicures help me stay calm."

Ryse smiled, "Well, maybe I need to start doing your routine because you seem very level headed."

"Yes, maybe we can make future plans once we see how this goes," Coby winked.

The hostess interrupted their conversing, "Well, I will take your belonging to your spa room and lead you two to the dining area for breakfast."

The two followed the hostess as she walked briskly to the dining area. In the large room, there was a private dining space set for the two of them. While other patrons were there as well, they had a closed-off area where the two of them could enjoy their dinner without interruption.

"I see you like things to be very exclusive?" Ryse scoffs.

"It's not that I prefer them to be exclusive, it just happens to be a habit. Dealing with celebrities all the time and always working on projects, there is a level of privacy you have to maintain. We usually don't give out details of projects we're working on until deals have been reached and contracts signed. Also, sometimes in production, you don't want too many details leaking until you're ready to launch."

"Yeah, I get that part. It's like with investment deals, with some of our big-name clients we have to keep things hush, especially with mergers and acquisitions."

"Exactly! And once you get used to doing things that way, it just becomes a way of life."

The waitress assigned to service Ryse and Coby makes her way to the table. She placed white linen napkins before them and then stood with her hands behind her back, "May I offer any morning beverages? Coffee? Juice? Mimosas?"

"We'll take coffee and mimosas, please?" Coby said without even letting Ryse order for herself. He then looked at Ryse, "Would you like any special creamer? Any particular champagne for your mimosa?"

Ryse chuckled, "Well, I'm glad you asked? I thought I was going to have to just take what was given to me," she said sarcastically. "Actually if you have mocha flavored creamer, I'd be delighted to have that. And I'll take a Moet and grapefruit juice mimosa."

Coby looked up at the waitress, "Yes, that is all, thank you."

"My pleasure. Be right back with your beverages, and the cooking servant will be around shortly to plate your table."

Coby watched the waitress walk away, then returned his gaze back to Ryse, "You're funny!"

Ryse's eyebrows raised and furrowed, "I'm funny? How you just gon' order for the both of us? How do you know I drink alcohol? How do you know I'm a coffee drinker?"

"I told you before that you need to sit back and let someone else lead. You're getting feisty because I ordered a drink for you? There's water on the table if you'd prefer to just drink that," Coby mocked.

"Of course, I don't just prefer to drink water. I'm just saying I didn't mind ordering for myself."

"Well, when you're with me, ladies don't have to worry about taking care of themselves. Let me handle those things."

Ryse rolled her eyes. She contemplated for a second to engage in a back and forth battle, but she decided to choose her wisely. She didn't feel it was worth it.

The waitress came back shortly with their coffee and mimosas, and the cooking servant arrived soon after that. The two filled up on bacon, eggs, croissants, and fruit before they were whisked away to the spa area.

Ryse was awed by the care that Coby set out for them to have an enjoyable experience during their couples massage session. There were lovely flowers everywhere, and the ambiance was set for a beyond common experience. They had a luxurious 120-minute massage followed by an indulging pedicure and manicure session. After the spa treatment, they grabbed a quick snack, and Coby checked them into a nearby hotel. They had two separate rooms, and he told Ryse to be ready in the lobby by 7pm.

Ryse enjoyed a nice quiet afternoon nap and then woke up to a full glam squad knocking on her hotel room door. She was enamored by the luxury that Coby was pouring onto her. She wasn't sure if it was his standard treatment that he gave to women or if it was because he really liked her. Whatever it was, she soaked up every moment of it.

Once Ryse was ready and put together, she thanked the glam squad for making her look fabulous, and she headed toward the hotel lobby. Ryse was stunning, as she made her way down the corridor. It was likened until the scene out of *Pretty Woman* where Julia Roberts adorned in her red dress, red lips, and hair up was walking with Richard Geer, and everyone was in awe of her transformation. All heads were turning to look at Ryse as she strutted in her silver, off the shoulder Chanel dress and matching heels.

She expected to be standing in the lobby waiting on Coby, as she was about five minutes ahead of schedule to meet in the lobby. But she was handsomely greeted by a well-dressed Coby, decked in a tailored Sean Jean black suit with a silver-gray necktie.

Ryse smiled as she walked toward him, "Hey, handsome."

Coby blushed and leaned in to kiss Ryse on the cheek as she stopped in front of him, "Hey, beautiful. You look even more beautiful than I expected."

Ryse blushed as well as they then turned toward the exit and was greeted by the same driver from the morning. They got in the town car and made their way toward Mae & Company restaurant. Upon arrival, they were greeted by the valet workers and escorted into the restaurant where the hostess, once again, recognized Coby and lead them to the private dining area for their dinner.

"This is amazing," Ryse exclaimed. She had never been to Mae & Company but only heard about it from friends and colleagues. As she sat down at the square white linen table, she looked around at the architecture and room décor. She took long gazes to commit to memory, not wanting to miss a single element.

"You like it?" Coby asked, interrupting her thoughts.

"Absolutely! I never would have imagined that this place would be filled with so much Black history. I mean, I heard about it, but to see it in person is breathtaking."

"Yes, Mae James, the matriarch the restaurant was named after, was big on African artifacts. She was one of the first successful millionaire entrepreneurs in Chicago, and anyone who followed her knew her love for African artifacts and how much she loved Black culture." Coby said elated to share the few bits of details he knew about the restaurant.

"Oh, my God! It reminds me of an even more upscale version of the legendary Cotton Club but redesigned with African art. I could live here!" Ryse cherished.

As they conversed, the waiter came to their table, showing the menu for the evening. It was a special select menu that was prepared, especially for them outside of the regular menu items.

Ryse looked over the menu and asked sarcastically, "So do I get to choose what I want to eat, or have you already done so?"

"The items you see here are special select items, you can order everything on the menu or just the items you want. Completely up to you!" Coby leaned back in his seat, not giving into her sarcasm.

Ryse ready for a fight was caught off guard by his unwillingness to amuse her banter, "Well, in that case, I'll take everything!" She said to the waiter and smiled.

"Of course, ma'am. And just so you know with the full course selection, everything will be in small bites to enjoy comfortably." He turns to Coby, "And for you, sir?"

"I'll have the same."

"My pleasure. Your complimentary champagne will arrive shortly. Is there any other beverage choices that you would like to have?" The waiter waits for their reply.

Ryse looked at Coby, waiting for him to answer.

"What? I'm shocked you didn't jump at the chance to answer for yourself," Coby said sarcastically.

"Well, I'm fine with champagne unless you want something else?"

Coby returned his eyes to the waiter, "No, that would be all for the beverages. Thank you!"

"My pleasure, sir." The waiter bows and then walked away from the table.

"Why are you always looking for a fight? Does that turn you on? Are you kinky in that way?" Coby asked.

"What?" Ryse jerked her head back and frowns, "What kind of question is that to ask someone? Why would that be considered kinky? And why did it have to go to sex that quickly?"

"I'm just trying to figure out why everything is a fight with you? I just want to show you a good time, and you keep trying to stop my pampering of you."

"Well, I'm not trying to stop you from pampering me, I just don't like people controlling me. I have one dad, I don't need another one," Ryse scoffed.

"Oh, I see what it is now. You're not used to a man taking care of you. You're too independent. Who scared you?"

"Scared me? Nobody! My dad just taught me not to depend on a man, and I want to make sure I make him proud."

"How old are you, Ryse?"

Ryse waved him off, "You shouldn't ask a lady her age."

Coby sat up in his seat, "No, seriously. How old are you?"

"33. Why?" Ryse asked reluctantly.

"You're a beautiful, successful woman. Has a good head on your shoulders. Very intelligent and still single. Why do you think that is?"

Ryse smacks her lips and takes a sip of the champagne from her glass, "Because I have standards, that's why."

"By no means am I telling you to lower your standards, but do you think some of those standards are getting in the way of you finding love?"

"Can we change the subject? You sound like Meghan."

Coby laughed, "Who is Meghan?"

"One of my good girlfriends. She's always badgering me about my love life. She seems to believe that some of the things that contribute to my lack of love are because *I'm too bossy*, as she would say."

"Well, you might want to re-evaluate her advice. No man wants a woman that won't submit."

Ryse folded her arms, "Oh my, well you sound really ancient with that ideology. Submission is an ugly word to me. We both should submit to one another. I'm just as equal in a relationship as the man. I bring to the table just as much as he does. Why should I be the only one to submit?" Ryse grabbed her glass of champagne with one hand and takes a sip while waving Coby off with the other.

Coby could tell that the subject was irritating Ryse. Just as he was about to go on with the conversation, the waiter arrives with their dinner.

"Oh, thank God!" Ryse said as she was done with the love life conversation.

As they prepared for dinner, Coby quickly grabbed Ryse's dinner napkin and placed it in her lap.

Ryse wanted to resist, but she sat back and allowed him to cover her. Then he quickly grabbed her dinner fork. Her eyes furrowed as she pondered what he was about to do with the fork. He then dug in her plate, picking up one of the sautéed Brussel sprouts on her plate.

"What are you doing, Coby?"

"Shhhhh," he said, placing his finger to his lips. He continued to load the Brussel sprout and then motioned it to her mouth. "Open up."

Ryse looked at Coby, she looked around wondering who was watching the scene, until quickly realizing that they were in a private dining area. She released her guard once again and opened her mouth. He softly placed the food in her mouth. She closed her mouth and pulled back, taking the Brussel sprout off the fork.

"Is it good?" Coby asked.

Ryse shook her head yes and stared deeply into Coby's eyes.

The Second Date

"Ooohhhh, baby! I'm so happy you enjoyed your date. Are you going to go on another one?" Mama Peaches said cheerfully on the other end of the receiver.

"Yeah, we actually have another one planned soon. It was a great experience. She's very challenging, though." Coby said hesitantly.

"What you mean, baby?"

"She's just challenging. Everything is a fight for her."

Mama Peaches cleared her throat, "Challenging? You could tell that from one date?"

"Mama Peaches, we spent nearly the entire day together. At breakfast, she got mad at me because I picked the beverages for us."

Mama Peaches laughed heartily, "Well, why are you going on a second date?"

Coby paused for a minute. "You know what? I guess because I just want to make sure. And I kinda like her."

"Well, that settles it. Where are you all going?"

"Nothing as elaborate as the first date, but something simple so that we can talk more. I arranged for a picnic lunch."

"Hmph. Well, that's different," Mama Peaches scoffed.

"What? You think she won't like it?" Coby became anxious.

"No. I won't say I don't think she wouldn't like it. I'm just saying it's different. You went from an all-day date to a polar opposite one. I guess this will test her character. How she reacts to it will determine if she is all about the flash or looking for something concrete."

"Woah, Mama Peaches. I'm not looking for a relationship. I'm just dating."

"Gent, please! You're looking for a relationship. Clara just knocked a little steam out of you, that's all. You were so ready to get married. I can tell you're looking for your special lady."

"Well, not this soon. I just met her. She's the first real date I've had in months. So we'll just see where this goes."

"OK, baby! Well Mama got to get these collards and roast going, Harold likes to eat at 5pm!"

Coby laughed, "Tell the old man I said hello, and I must get myself ready as well to pick up Ryse for our date."

They both ended the call, and Coby walked to his bathroom and started the shower. Just as he was getting ready to get in the shower, he hears his cellphone ringing. He rushed out of the bathroom, half-naked to see who was calling. As he checked the caller ID, he was surprised to see it was Ryse.

"Hello?" Coby answered.

"Hey, how are you? It's Ryse," she said enthusiastically.

"Hey. Is everything OK? You're not canceling on me, are you?"

Ryse let out a boastful howl, "No, silly. I was calling to see if I could meet you at your home? I had to run out and take care of something, and I just figured instead of going all the way back home, I can just come to you."

"Uhhhh, sure. I guess it's OK."

Ryse sensed his uncomfortableness, "Are you sure?"

"Yeah, I'm sure. It just caught me off guard."

"OK, well what's the address?"

"5514 Robert Court. When you get to the gate, tell the guard your name, and he will let you enter. My home is last home at the end of the cul-de-sac." There was a long pause, Coby couldn't hear Ryse's response. "Hello?" Coby called out.

"Oh, I'm sorry, I'm here. I was putting the address in the GPS. I'm actually not too far from you. GPS says I'm twenty minutes away," Ryse said hurriedly. "Guard? You have a guard? Oh, you live in a gated community?"

"Well, I am the president of UCC…"

"Right, right. I'm sorry."

"OK, well I was right in the middle of showering, so let me tell the guard your name and let the maid know you'll be arriving soon."

"OK, see you soon."

Coby quickly ended the call and yelled out to Stephanie, his housemaid. Stephanie quickly emerged from around a corner, "Yes, Mr. St. Williams?"

"I have a young lady, Ryse Taylor, coming to visit very soon. Can you call down to the front gate and let them know she'll be arriving. It's Ryse, R. Y. S. E., Taylor."

Stephanie frowned up her face with slight concern, "You have a lady visitor?"

Coby rolled his eyes, "Yes, Stephanie. I have a lady visitor. The young lady that won the date with me from the bachelor auction."

Stephanie lifts her hands in surrender, "OK, I'm not judging, just surprised. Just wasn't expecting to see anyone come around here so soon after Clara."

"Don't start! Thanks, Stephanie, can I get ready now?"

Stephanie chuckled and exited the room.

Coby went back to his bathroom and disrobed fully and got into the shower. After a 10 minute shower he went into his walk-in closet a found some picnic-worthy clothing and groomed himself putting on body lotion and cologne. As he was putting on his facial lotion and brushing his beard, Stephanie came into the room.

"Mr. St. Williams, your lovely guest has arrived," Stephanie said, calling out with a broad grin.

"Lovely, huh?" Coby said to Stephanie, watching her through the reflection of the mirror.

"Yes, quite lovely. More lovely than I expected."

"Is that so, Stephanie?"

Stephanie laughed again and left the room.

Coby put the last finishing touches on his appearance and then went down into the sitting area where Stephanie usually escorted guests to. As Coby entered into the sitting room, he found Ryse standing looking at the paintings that were displayed on the wall.

"You like those?" Coby said startling Ryse.

Ryse jumped, and clutched her chest, "Oh, you scared me," she chuckled. "Yes, they are beautiful. I appreciate good Black art. I have a few paintings of my own in my home. I see we have a bit more in common than I originally thought."

Coby raised his eyebrows, "What's that supposed to mean?"

"Exactly how I said it."

Coby rolled his eyes, "Well, are you ready? You look great by the way."

"Yes, I'm ready. Where are we going?"

"Well, I thought I'd plan a lunch picnic so that we can get a bit more acquainted with each other. We didn't do much talking on our first date."

"Oh, OK. Well before we leave do you mind if I can get a tour? Your home is beautiful."

"A tour? Sure."

Ryse grabbed her purse from the sofa and followed Coby's lead. He showed her his massive six-bedroom, seven-bath home with a full entertained area and his large backyard and pool area. As they toured the backyard area, Ryse was consumed by the immaculate gardening and decking area.

"Instead of having a picnic somewhere else, why don't we have it right here in your backyard?" Ryse asked as she was admiring the area.

"Here? Are you sure? Because I had things pretty planned out. I had the chef schedule to come and meet us there in the next two hours."

"So the chef can't come here? I'm sure there's enough time to tell him that there is a change in plans."

Coby thought to himself to reflect a bit, "Well, I guess that would work." He pulled out his cellphone and began to scroll through his contacts. He pressed a button and then puts the phone to his ear and waited for a few seconds. "Hey, Carlos! How are you?" There was a pause, and he looked at Ryse. "Oh, no, there's no problem. Just a change of plans. I'm going to do the picnic at my home in the backyard." Coby laughed, "Yes, I'm sure. It was actually a suggestion by the guest." One last pause and then Coby smiled, "OK! Yes, same time. See you soon."

Coby pulled down the phone from his ear and pressed a button to lock the phone and then he put it in his pocket. He then looked at Ryse, and they both smiled.

"Well, now that we have that sorted out, let's have a seat and chat," Ryse summoned.

Ryse walked to the nearby patio furniture and sat down. Coby shrugged and followed her lead and sat down.

"Uhmmm, how are you hijacking this entire date? Glad I didn't have any other surprise planned. Otherwise, you would have ruined it," Coby scoffed.

"Oh, I'm sorry. I really didn't mean any harm. I was just looking at this beautiful scenery, and I thought that it would be a great idea to just stay here. I actually feel very comfortable here."

"Do you? I guess my interior designer did her job correctly."

"Yeah, I guess so," Ryse said charmingly.

The two conversed talking about a range of topics from their childhoods growing up in Southlake Park and the colleges they both attended. They spoke about their parents and what they do in their companies on a more individual level.

The chef arrived and prepared for them lobster tails and crab legs with shrimp cocktail. Grilled chicken was also on the menu with mixed fruit and home-style potato salad. Coby always tried to incorporate rooted elements into his life. As he would often repeat Mama Peaches old saying, "Life isn't only about where you're going. It's about not forgetting where you came from," into his lifestyle.

Coby always tried to hire Black first before any other race when he would start new projects and even amongst his staff. He was actually more down-to-earth than he appeared to others, and Ryse was beginning to see that quality in Coby. She often found herself caught in his words as he spoke about how he secured his deal for his network and the ups and downs of Black television programming.

By the time lunch was over, they had found that they had been talking for hours. Ryse was pooped, "Wow, I'm stuffed and could use a nap!"

"I know, right? Well, you're welcome to nap in one of the guest rooms if you like. I don't have any plans today and had planned on coming back home after our date was over."

"That sounds nice. But why don't we Netflix and chill... or better yet, UCC and chill?" Ryse said chuckling.

Coby's eyebrows raised, "UCC and chill, huh?"

"The PG-13 version, though," Ryse quickly rebutted.

"Got ya'," Coby responded and winked.

Coby lead them down to the entertainment area where there was a large projection screen displayed on the wall. Coby grabbed a remote and pressed a few buttons and appeared was one of the popular television shows airing on UCC.

They each sat in a recliner-style theater seat and leaned back. It wasn't long before both of them had fallen fast asleep. After an hour nap, Coby found himself awaken by the touch of Ryse's hand going up and down his arm. He opened his eyes and looked over at Ryse. Her eyes were still closed, and it appeared that she was in a state of light sleep.

As Coby watched over her, he was drawn to her beauty as he concentrated on her face, looking at her eyebrows, her almond-shaped eyes, her tiny button nose, and curvy lips. Without hesitation, he leaned over and softly kissed Ryse.

Coby pulled back, and Ryse opened her eyes, smiled, and leaned in, and kissed him back. As they deeply embraced, Coby lifted up the seat divider so that they could get closer and their kisses became more passionate. Ryse felt fluid in the romance of it all. She could faintly hear the television program in the background and became engulfed in the deep kisses.

Suddenly Ryse stopped and pulled back from Coby, "Wait a minute! What's happening?"

Coby was stunned and looked confused, "I don't know. Whatever you want to happen."

Ryse's eyes went back and forth between both Coby's eyes, and then she aggressively started to kiss him again. It had been months since she been intimate with a man and she suddenly had a flashback of her lady parts thumping when she first saw Coby on the stage at the bachelor's auction.

She began to remove the polo shirt he had on, and he went to unbuckle her belt and unzipped her pants. As Ryse's pants began to come down, she climbed on top of Coby, breathing very heavily. The passion consumed them both, and they allowed for nature to take its course.

The War

After the second date, things between Coby and Ryse escalated very quickly. Their budding spring romance flourished into a hot summer escapade, but soon the war would begin.

Ryse soon found herself falling heavily for Coby. The high energy chase that they both gave each other was like a challenge for her – one that she was driven to conquer. While she was happy that Coby would give her all of his time when he was free, there was one main issue that Ryse had. She was unhappy that their courtship had to remain private.

Just like all the private dates they've explored throughout the relationship, Ryse was unable to tell the world about this new love in her life. As Coby introduced Ryse into his world, she had to do it at a distance. He would invite her to industry parties, but she was unable

to be photographed with him. He always encouraged her

to bring a plus one with her so that she wouldn't be alone

at events. This started to bother Ryse, as yet again she

was at an industry party and could only watch her man

from a distance.

"Stop staring at him!" Meghan said as she stood

in her all-black evening gown, holding a glass of

champagne.

"Why does he even invite me to these things?

This is so embarrassing. I feel like a side chick." Ryse was

very agitated as she threw back her entire glass of

champagne in one gulp. Coby and Ryse made eye contact

for a quick second. He looked her up and down as she

was beautiful and her cream-colored, sequin floor length

gown. She rolled her eyes at him.

"Well, at least he's inviting you. And don't feel like a side chick. I think he's making sure you come to these events, so you'll know that you're his lady."

"Well, if I'm his lady then why can't anyone know about us?"

"Do you want cameras in your face all the time? Do you want your privacy invaded? Because that's what's going to happen as soon as the public catches wind that you're the woman to Mr. UCC himself," Meghan jeered.

Ryse focused her attention onto Meghan, "Yeah, you're right."

Ryse sighed and then summoned one of the cocktail waitresses over to give her another glass of champagne. Just as she was getting her other drink, Ryse sees a very attractive lady walk up to Coby and give him a hug. She remembers seeing her before at a different party.

Ryse continued to watch their interaction. The mystery lady rubbed Coby's shoulders and caressed his arms. Meghan noticed the lady as well.

"Who is that?" Meghan asked.

"I don't know," Ryse snarled. She went into her small evening bag and pulled out her cellphone. She began to type quickly. *Uhmm, sir? What the hell? Who is that? And why is she touching you like that?* She pressed send and looked up to Coby's direction waiting for him to respond.

As Ryse watched Coby, she saw him grab his right pants pocket. She assumed that he felt his phone vibrating in his pocket and was touching it to make sure. He smiled at the mystery lady and then pulled out his cellphone. Ryse watched intently from her place.

Still smiling, he unlocked his phone and began to read the message. His facial expression went from a bright smile to an awkward smile. He looked up and cased the room to see if he could find Ryse. Suddenly as he looked straight ahead, he was able to location Ryse and locked eyes with her. He then turned his attention to his phone and responded back. *This is a harmless associate, Ryse. I know her husband. Nothing to be worried about.* He pressed send and returned his attention back to the lady.

Ryse felt her phone vibrate and she looked down at his reply, she was livid. "I can't do this!" Ryse mumbled to herself.

"What's wrong? What did he say?" Meghan asked, concerned.

"He's talking about that's a friend's wife. I wonder if her husband knows she's that friendly with other men?"

"Do you trust him?"

Ryse looked at Meghan with confusion, "What?"

"Do you trust him? It doesn't seem like you do."

"I don't know what I trust. This is the first guy that I've liked in a long time and no one, besides you, knows he's my man. I don't know why it bothers me, it just does." Ryse started to become emotional out of nowhere.

"OK, OK! You all need to communicate," Meghan said, giving her friend a consoling hug.

Ryse looked back down at her phone and sent Coby another message. *We need to talk. This secrecy you wish to have is not working for me anymore.*

Ryse watched Coby from across the room, read the text, and then he rolled his eyes and blew out raspberries. She saw the mystery lady express concern for whatever was troubling him and Coby hugged her and walked away. Ryse followed with her eyes until he left out of the room.

"Let's go!" Ryse said to Meghan.

Meghan responded in a whinny voice, "Why? We just got here. I was hoping to network a bit more."

"Well if you want to stay that's fine. I'll take an Uber home."

"Uber? Girl, you're acting like a brat."

"Whatever!" Ryse said as she waved off Meghan.

Meghan didn't go chasing after Ryse either. She allowed her to go walking off pouting like a little baby. Ryse made her way to the venue lobby and sat down as she contemplated calling the Uber. She looked down at her phone, scrolling through social media when she felt a body sit down next to her. She looked up to see it was Coby. She didn't say a word but rolled her eyes.

"Now, don't do that," Coby said.

"You dismissed me as if you don't care how I feel."

"You're paranoid for no reason."

Ryse eyes grew wide, and she placed her hand over her heart, "Paranoid? Really? How would you like it if some mystery man was all touchy-feely on me? No one knows we're together so I could be one of many women in this place who is dating you."

"Ryse, you are trippin'," Coby said, becoming agitated.

"Excuse me?"

"You heard me. You're trippin'. You're saying things as if you don't know me."

Ryse chuckled sarcastically, "I don't know you!"

Coby was offended, "You don't know me?"

"No," Ryse responded nonchalantly.

"You don't know me?" Coby asked again just to be sure Ryse heard him.

"No. I don't know you," Ryse responded sassy-like.

"How long have we been seeing each other?"

Ryse sat and thought for a minute, "Uhm, I don't know. Maybe like five months."

"And in these five months, you're saying you don't know me?"

Ryse peered at Coby sternly, "If you ask me that question one more time!"

"What is the problem, Ryse?"

"I need to feel confident that I'm your lady if that is what I am to you."

"You are my lady, but right now is just not the time to go public with our relationship," Coby sighed.

"Why not?" Ryse's voice was slightly elevated.

Coby looked around to see if anyone was paying attention to their conversation, "Lower your voice, please!"

"Oh, right! We don't want anyone to get the hint that we are together, right?" Ryse rolled her eyes.

"It's just not the right time. I have some huge projects for the network that will be launching soon, and I don't need extra press circulation about my love life distracting from the releases."

"Oh, so now I'm a distraction?"

Coby palmed his face, "That is not what I said, Ryse."

"Practically, it is."

Coby quickly gets up, "I don't have time for this. You want to make something more than what it is. I'm trying to tell you my why, and you're turning this into a situation to where you're the victim."

Ryse jumped up after Coby and grabbed his arm. "Where are you going?" She asked sternly.

Coby turned around and looked at her hand around his arm. "I'm going back to the party. You enjoy the rest of your evening."

Coby walked away while Ryse watched in disgust. She couldn't believe what just happened. She went on to order her Uber and left the party.

The Love

The war between Coby and Ryse lasted another three months. Coby was continually persistent that their love is kept a secret, while Ryse was adamant about the world knowing that Coby was her man.

Ryse really couldn't explain where the obsession about it was coming from. It was almost like a being kid who is told they couldn't do something and out of rebellion they do it anyway. Their summer romance was turning into a fall conundrum. Meghan kept inquiring to her about why she was still in relations with Coby if she was so upset about the privacy of their relationship. Ryse didn't really have an answer to the question.

Ryse continued to be the secret invitee to all of Coby's significant events and then also continued to make private scenes with him when her jealousy would show its face. They would often leave the events in their separate cars and then end up at one of the other's place and make passionate love. They were magnetically drawn to each other despite the turmoil they were experiencing.

While their romance was continually growing confrontational, Coby decided that it was time they got away. He planned a last minute trip for the both of them to Aruba. Coby flew out a day earlier to avoid being seen traveling with Ryse.

Since the launch of the new network programs, the press was everywhere, and he was in all the magazine for their fall issues. His low profile was essential to the success of the new programs because he wanted the actors and hosts to get most of the press media.

"Hey, girl! Just calling to let you know I made it here safe. I just got off the phone with my mother. I'll see you all in a couple of days," Ryse said to Meghan.

"Well, you enjoy your vacation and try not to argue with Coby about you know what. I'm sure he planned a beautiful trip for you two."

"Yeah, you're right. I'm going to try and enjoy it. But I feel like he's just trying to distract me from the obvious."

Meghan sighed, "Girl, what do you want him to do? Put out a big press release that says, *I'm dating the beautiful Ryse Taylor?* Girl, stop it."

"I'm trying! I really am! But I'm going to talk to you later, the car is here to take me to the villa."

"Ok, love. Enjoy yourself!"

They ended the call, and Ryse was escorted into the vehicle. The driver drove down a scenic, ocean view lined road. Ryse was enjoying the beauty of it all and in anticipation of seeing Coby. She hadn't seen him in about a week due to their busy schedules, so she was excited to reunite. The driver soon pulled up to a colossal villa with beautiful palm trees, lush grass, and an ocean as the swimming pool. She was in awe.

The driver pulled around the circular driveway where she was greeted by a smiling Coby. He had his tan Bermuda shorts on with a predictive white cotton polo shirt and tan casual shoes. Upon the car stopping, the driver quickly gets out and runs to the passenger side of the car and let's Ryse out.

She emerged from the car in a floor-length, form-fitting, striped black and white dress which was also had longed-sleeved. She had just gotten her hair braided for the trip, so her butt-length box braids flowed in the soft wind. She smiled brightly when she saw Coby.

Coby walked smoothly over to her and kissed her passionately while grabbing her butt tightly and pulling her into him. "Ohhh, I've missed you," he said in between kisses.

"Baby, I missed you, too." Ryse pulled away from Coby and took in more of the scene. "This is such a beautiful villa. I don't think I've ever been anywhere as beautiful as this."

"I'm glad you like it."

As the driver retrieved Ryse's luggage and followed the two into the villa, he leaves the bags in the foyer of the villa. He waited quietly for Coby to dismiss him as he watched the two embraced in another steamy kiss.

One of the maids comes and retrieves the luggage from the driver, and then Coby walked over to him and handed him a tip. "That is all we need for today, Rich. You have our itinerary for the weekend, so we'll see you tomorrow morning."

The driver takes the tip from Coby and tips his hat to him, "My pleasure, Mr. St. Williams. See you in the morning."

"Thank you, sir!" Coby said back.

Coby then joined Ryse on the back patio as she was relaxing in one of the lounge chairs looking over the ocean. Ryse reached out her hand, suggesting that Coby holds it. He softly grabbed her hand and smiled.

Ryse breathes in the air, "Oh my. This air is so fresh! I could live here forever!"

"I know. Isn't it wonderful? I've thought about getting a vacation home here, but with my busy schedule I don't think I'd have enough time to get my money's worth."

"Yeah, that's true. But I know one thing's for sure, I'll definitely be back here to enjoy this gorgeous weather."

"I'm glad you love it," Coby said as he released his grip from Ryse and leaned back in the lounge chair.

"So what's on the menu for dinner? I'm so hungry. All I had was breakfast before the flight," Ryse said, rubbing her stomach.

"They didn't serve lunch on the plane?"

"Yes, they did, but I was asleep. I was pretty exhausted. The firm has been busy the past week. I've been working plenty of late nights ensuring that some major deals closed before this trip."

"Well, I can understand the exhaustion. I'm thrilled that we're done with promo season myself. The constant interviewing and press all in your face everywhere you turn was draining."

"So, what's for dinner?"

"An exquisite meal! Lemon-buttered salmon and filet mignon and whatever else the chef prepares with it."

"That sounds delicious, and I don't even know what else I'm eating." They both laughed and enjoyed the ocean wave sounds as they both drifted off into a quick nap before dinner.

Soon they transitioned to freshening up for dinner as the aromas from the exquisite meal filled the air. Beautifully crusted lemon-buttered salmon and caramelized-seared filet mignon, with buttery garlic mashed potatoes, fresh green beans, and sautéed spinach. While at the dinner table, they both gazed into each other's eyes while eating and sipping their champagne.

Love swirled around in the air. Ryse was finding herself becoming suffocated with the euphoria of love that was Coby. Ryse pushed back from her place setting and grabbed Coby's hand and guided him to their master bedroom suite. She sat him on the bed and began to unbutton his striped blue and green shirt and began to kiss him intently upon the neck.

Coby kissed Ryse back on her neck, lips, and shoulders as his hands slip up her thighs underneath her thigh-length cotton cami-dress. As he pulled her underwear down to her ankles, she pushed him back slightly and straddled Coby. Her hands find their way to his belt buckle, and she began to release him from his pants.

They passionately French kissed as they lie naked in the bed having the best love making session they ever had throughout their entire relationship. If Ryse wasn't sure by then, that very moment solidified her feelings for Coby.

As they engaged fervently, Coby gently turned Ryse onto her back and gets atop her. He lovingly entered into her and Ryse exploded with love. Her hands caressed his smooth back, and then she cuffed his backside. In that very moment, they both belonged to each other. Coby discovered himself wrapped into Ryse's essence and he couldn't break away.

They climaxed into a soul-tying bliss and laid in each other's arms as they listened to the sounds of the waves crashing into the shore.

"I love you, Coby," Ryse whispered.

"I love you, too, Ryse."

This was the first time that either of them would say the words to each other. They both spent so much time attempting to control the relationship that they never took the time to acknowledge the love that was growing between them.

Ryse was so focused on everyone knowing the Coby was her man that she didn't enjoy the moments that she had with him. Had she done so, she would have been able to see how much he cared for her. How he treated her so delicately when he was with her. He wanted to be her protector, her confidant, her lover. He tried to offer her something that she hadn't had in a long time. He wanted to be her security. Not security in a materialistic way, but security in love. She couldn't see that at first. But after the lovemaking session, she was starting to see the light.

Just as they were nestling into each other's scent, both of their phones began to simultaneously chime continually. Notification after notification, their phones sounded.

"What the heck?" Ryse sat up, looking confused.

Coby followed right behind her, "What's going on?"

They both quickly jumped out of bed and grabbed their phones, respectively.

As Ryse opened her phone, she noticed that she had about one hundred and fifty Twitter notifications and over two hundred Facebook notifications. Her eyebrows furrowed, and then she went to her text messages. There was one from Meghan. *Girl, look at this!!!* The text read with an accompanying image.

It was a screenshot of a post by Southlake Park News' social media page, the headline read, "Meet Mr. Jacob St. Williams' New Love." And there right in Ryse's face was an image of her and Coby from earlier that day greeting each other as she arrived at the villa.

Ryse covered her mouth in shock. She looked at Coby, as she expected he had been sent some of the same news. "How did they get this?!"

"I knew this was going to happen. The press is so sneaky," Coby said with a smirk on his face.

"But how? This is from today!"

"Ain't technology something? I'm sure they have been following both of us."

"They? Following? What are you talking about, Coby?" Ryse was flabbergasted.

"The press is watching, even when you think they're not."

Coby quickly clicked on the news article post and saw multiple images of Ryse and Coby at different events. The reporter went on to talk about how she noticed that Ryse was at all of the major events hosted by Coby and UCC. The reporter talked about how she saw that they would always end up in some corner together, having inconspicuous conversations. The last and final burden of proof was them meeting up together in Aruba.

Ryse was outdone, "You mean to tell me they followed us all the way here to Aruba? How in the hell would they know where we're going?"

"You see, this is why I didn't want us to go public." As Coby was speaking, both their phones continued to chime with notifications from their social media accounts. Ryse couldn't handle it, so she turned off her phone. Coby laughed out loud.

"What's so funny?" Ryse asked.

"You. You wanted this, and now it's out there. I'm not mad, though. I guess I'm glad I don't have to argue with you about it anymore." Coby continued to laugh as he was making fun of Ryse. Now she realized the severity of dating a celebrity.

"It's not funny, Coby. I'm weirded out by the fact that some person can follow me across the country just for a news article. That is creepy! What is the reporter getting out of this?"

"She's getting the recognition of breaking a new story. No worries, as long as we stay private all they'll have is pictures."

Ryse continued to stare at Coby in total shock, "Unbelievable. I just never imagined. I guess now I really understand how famous you are."

"Well, I'm not that famous. Just famous enough to be a targeted source for a good news story. Don't worry. If we stay private enough, we will fall off their radar, and they will move on to someone else."

"Are you sure, Coby?"

"I hope so," he said not so confidently.

Ty Young

The Battle

After Aruba things did began to settle down with the press on a public level, but privately Ryse was having a hard time adjusting to the constant attention from those that followed her on social media and reporters calling to get Ryse to confirm her relationship with Coby.

Meghan tried to warn her initially, but Ryse didn't fully grasp the concept of dating someone in the of the public eye. Ryse's quiet, cozy upper-middle-class neighborhood was now turned into a place where the paparazzi would stakeout, and an occasional fan or two would linger around hoping to meet Coby.

While she wasn't quite at the Beyoncé level of fame when it came to fans, the media sure wasn't letting her off so quickly. Coby and Ryse had been photographed together at events after the initial story broke, but neither had yet to make an official statement about the status of their relationship.

Ryse was annoyed by the lack of privacy she was now faced with, and this seemed to cause tension in their relationship. She rarely wanted to go out anymore, and much of her anger about the situation was displaced toward Coby.

Her firm was bombarded by media at times, and some of her employees became annoyed by the media attention as well.

Ryse was in the lobby of her firm as she waited for Coby to pick her up. They were headed off to another event, this time a film premiere of a movie that one of the actors of one of Coby's network's new shows was staring in.

Instead of having the glam squad come to her home, she had them prep her at her office. She didn't want media disturbing her neighbors.

As Coby pulled up to her firm, the paparazzi appeared out of nowhere flashing cameras at his car hoping to get a good picture of him. He didn't step out of the car nor raised down the window. Soon as Ryse sees the car pull up, two bodyguards walked up to her.

"Ms. Taylor, are you ready?" One of the burly bodyguards said to her.

"Yes, as ready as I'm going to be. I think I should be getting used to this by now."

The bodyguard chuckled, "Goes with the territory, I guess. Well, let's get you out here and through this crowd."

As soon as the other guard opens the door, immediately the photographers and reporters swarmed the area.

"Ms. Taylor, when are you going to reveal your relationship with Jacob St. Williams?" One reporter yelled out.

"Ms. Taylor, can you confirm that you were with Mr. Williams in Aruba?" Another reporter yelled out to her from the crowd.

Ryse held her head down as she was barricaded by the two bodyguards. She could hear the flash of the cameras and the equipment touching sounds as everyone was battling to get a photo of her up-close.

"Watch it, watch it!" The bodyguard said as he strong-armed his way through photographers the short distance to the car.

As she was approaching the car, another reporter yelled out to her, "Ms. Taylor, is that Mr. St. Williams waiting for you in the car?"

The bodyguard opened the passenger door and gently pushed Ryse into the car. The car door slammed, and Ryse fell back into the seat. "Oh my, God!" Ryse yelled out.

Coby looked over to her and rubbed her arm, "I'm sorry, baby! Hopefully, all of this dies down soon."

"You keep saying that, Coby. It's been two months! When is it going to happen?"

"Woah, don't yell at me! I didn't ask for this, but now that it's here we just have to deal with it."

Ryse shook her head and tears began to well up in her eyes, "Quick, please give me some tissue. I do not want to mess up my makeup."

Coby quickly reached into the glove compartment and pulled out a pack of Kleenex and promptly handed them to Ryse. She frantically opened the package and dabbed under her eyes softly. Coby then drove away.

"I don't think I can handle this anymore," Ryse said stoically.

"C'mon, babe. It's not that bad."

"Not that bad?" Ryse scoffed and pulled the sun visor down as she looked in the mirror, "You're used to this, but I'm not. I honestly didn't think that things would get like this."

"So you're saying that you don't want to go to the premiere?"

"No, I'm not saying that. I will follow through with the premiere, but maybe we should take a break until the press dies down."

Coby came to a red light and looked at Ryse in disbelief. "Take a break? Are you serious?"

"Yes, I'm very serious. I've been thinking about this for a while now. I'm not sure I can handle this."

"For a while now? I thought you loved me?"

"I do love you, Coby. I do. But my entire life right now has been turned upside down. I get so many people contacting me. I feel like I have no control over my life. People track me down to the grocery store, meet me at my house. This type of harassment should be illegal!"

Coby sighed, "OK, I understand how you feel, but I assure you that you have nothing to worry about. If you could just ride out this storm, I can assure you that things will get better."

Ryse turned to Coby and touched the side of his cheek, "Baby, I'm sorry. I didn't mean to get you all upset right before the premiere. Let's just enjoy this night and talk about it later."

Coby soon pulled up to the movie premiere valet area so that they could walk the long red carpet. As they got out of the car, the paparazzi was sure to bombard them with many questions. The valet driver took Coby's keys and gave him a ticket and Coby joined Ryse on the red carpet.

As they began to walk the carpet, Coby attempted to grab Ryse's hand, but she slightly pulled away. They didn't walk the red carpet like they were a couple but walked it as if they were just friends. Ryse played her part, however. She knew to smile, she waved to the cameras and then suddenly disappeared into the movie theater.

"Really, Ryse?" Coby said irritated.

"What?"

"So you can't hold my hand now?"

"No, that's not it. I just wanted to minimize the questions. Don't you think it would be easier that way?" Ryse smiled at a woman that walked by and said hi to her and Coby.

"Ryse, they already have us in multiple pictures cuddled up. Remember Aruba?"

Ryse pulled Coby to the side out of earshot of others, "Coby, why can't you respect my wishes? When I wanted to be public, you forced me to do it your way. So, just as I had to do it your way now let's try things my way."

"Well, at least with my way, we weren't taking breaks," he said annoyed.

"Coby, it's not permanent. I just need a moment to gather myself around all of this. You've had plenty of time to deal with the public."

"You know what? Whatever, Ryse. Have it your way. I'm done fighting with you."

Coby walked away and left Ryse standing in the concession area of the theater. Ryse quickly followed behind him, and they took their seats in the auditorium.

They barely spoke words to each other during the entire movie and even during the ride back to Coby's house was quiet. As they walked through the foyer, Coby was visibly irritated. He dropped his keys in the bowl sitting on the decorative stand and walked to the living room and turned on the television.

"So, you're not talking to me?" Ryse asked.

"What's there to talk about? You've made up your mind," Coby said while he pouted like a fourteen-year-old girl.

"Coby, I didn't say I wanted to break up, just wanted to take a break."

"Can you please explain to me what the difference is?"

"A break is just getting some space. A break up is when we declare our relationship is over. I don't want us to be over." Ryse walked over to the sofa and tried to touch Coby's face.

He jerked away from her and softly pushed her away, "Ryse, get away from me."

"Really, Coby?"

"Yes, get away from me. I'll sleep in one of the guest rooms tonight." Coby got up and walked away.

As Coby walked away, Ryse stood up from the couch angrily. "Don't worry. You can sleep in your own bed, I'll go home!" She yelled into Coby's direction.

Coby laughed out loud, "Really, Ryse? You know an Uber can't come into the complex. What are you going to do? Walk all the way to the gate and wait there for the Uber? I'm sure Jim will keep you company down there."

Ryse sat and thought for a minute. Coby was right. She really didn't feel like walking down to the entrance gate, and it was a little chilly outside. "Whatever!" She yelled out.

"I'll take you home in the morning." They both retreated to their separate rooms.

Ryse woke up the next morning in Coby's giant king size bed all alone. Right before going to bed, she grabbed one of Coby's expensive bottles of champagne and drank the entire bottle alone. She had a banging headache and felt a bit hungover.

She grabbed the overnight bag that she had there and went into the bathroom. She started the shower to allow it to get steamy. She stood watching herself in the mirror, and as the steam began to fill the bathroom, the tears started to flow out of her eyes. She realized that she just broke up with her man and she knew it was no way to take it back at that point.

After letting a few tears drop, Ryse quickly wiped her face, began brushing her teeth, and then washed her face with soap. You put her shower cap on and then got in the shower. She let the steamy water run down her face and body. All of a sudden, she felt a wave of depression sweep over her, and then she started to cry again.

Meanwhile, Coby was in his study talking on the phone with Mama Peaches. She had become his confidant when it came to women. She is the woman that helped him get over Clara when she broke things off with him.

"Mama Peaches, why does this keep happening to me?" Coby said with tremendous melancholy.

"Oh, gent, I don't know. But from what I gather about Ryse is that the break is not what she really wants. I think she just needs some time to think."

"But what if that time turns into us not being together at all?"

"Well, then that's how it meant to be. But I wouldn't stress myself too much about it. You have much more to focus on right now."

"I thought she would be the one."

"Really?" Mama Peaches was surprised to hear that.

"Yes, absolutely. She's smart, established in her business, and knows what she wants. As I think about settling down, she meets all of the checklists."

"I hear you, gent, maybe you need to just sit back and allow this space to help you get more clear on the direction you want to go with Ryse. If after some time she is still on your mind, if she hasn't reached out to you, call her!"

Coby sighed, "OK, if you say so."

"I know it hurts but let things flow naturally."

"Well, let me let you go. Let me check to see if she's up so I can take her home."

"OK, gent! I will talk to you later!" Mama Peaches said as she blew kisses in the phone receiver.

Coby hung up his cellphone and then got up to walk to see where Ryse was. As he walked through the kitchen toward the stairs, he found Ryse sitting at the kitchen bar waiting on him.

They both locked eyes. "Hi," Ryse said sadly.

"Hi."

"Well, I guess it's time for me to go home, huh?"

"That's if you want to go home."

Ryse stared into Coby's eyes and started to cry again. All she could think about was what would happen if she let Coby walk out of her life. Coby rushed over to Ryse and hugged her.

"Why the tears? This what you wanted, right?" Coby asked.

"I want the invasion of privacy to go away, not you. I was angry last night. I didn't mean it."

"Words have consequences, Ryse."

Ryse looked up at Coby, confused, "What do you mean?"

"I mean, breaking things off like that gave me flashbacks of when my ex, Clara, just upped and broke things off with me. How soon will it be before you start having issues with the paparazzi again?"

"Coby?"

"Ryse, like you said it will be just a break, right? This time apart will help us truly decide if we're meant for each other."

"Coby, c'mon, now. I didn't mean it. I was having a moment, that's all."

"Ryse, seriously, it's OK."

"Coby! No, it's not OK. You're just trying to get me back."

"No, I'm not. That's childish, I wouldn't play games like that, especially with a woman that I love."

Ryse smirked her face and jerked her head back, "If you love me, you wouldn't be doing this."

"Exactly! If you loved me, we wouldn't be here right now. You wouldn't have said what you said last night if you really loved me."

Ryse walked away bitterly. She aggressively picked up her bags and walked toward the front of Coby's house, "Fine, fine! That's the way you want it? Fine! Let's just go, please!"

Coby grabbed his keys, and they both got into his car that sat in the driveway, and Coby quickly pulled off. The ride was silent the entire time.

Once Coby pulled up to Ryse's house, she didn't say a word, she just got out of the car and slammed the door. Ryse was hot, and she couldn't even stand to look at Coby.

Coby watched Ryse walk to the front door and waited for her to get into the home safely. He sat outside her house for a few minutes and then he drove off. Coby drove away to a nearby hotel and sat in the lounge to have a drink. He sat for the next two hours, wondering if he made a mistake or not.

He was too hurt to admit that Ryse had bruised his ego a bit. He couldn't allow her to take control of the relationship in that way. Also, he wouldn't give another woman the satisfaction of walking out of his life on her own doing. In a way, he was making Ryse pay for what Clara did to him.

The Bitter Battle

Ryse and Coby's break up could have been summed up in a Mary J. Blige song. What was supposed to be a short break ended up being a nasty, media filled drama in the press. Ryse could not forgive Coby for going along with the short break. So when Coby attempted to come back with her, Ryse gave him the cold shoulder. As the press began to notice that they saw less of Coby and Ryse together, and more of Coby with different women, Ryse was becoming even more annoyed. Coby became bitter, and so did Ryse.

As the holidays passed, the more the two became bitter with one another. Thanksgiving, Christmas, right through to New Year's they would exchange ugly private dissatisfactions with the other's actions.

During their courtship, Ryse had become friends with a few people in Coby's circle, so she still found herself invited to the major industry parties, to which she would show up to out of spite toward Coby. She also never escaped the press. With each new woman Coby was photographed with, came another phone call or inquiry from the media to Ryse of how she felt about it.

The two didn't make it a clean split either. In between their annoyance for each other, somehow they would find their way back into each other's bed for drunken sex. Coby never took Ryse's name off of the approved guest list of the gated community, so after she'd had one too many, she'd somehow make her way to Coby's home. He would reluctantly let her in and then get lost her essence.

Neither wanted to admit the love that they still had for each other. They would have rather continued the bitter battle between them then reconcile. They embarrassed each other equally at the most recent soiree they were invited to.

"Meghan, is he looking over here at me?" Ryse asked as she wiped imaginary lent from her tight black dress.

Meghan looked up at the ceiling and then at Ryse, "I'm so sick of you two."

"What?"

"Why play this game? Both of you are acting like teenagers. Clearly, you're still in love with him, and he in love with you. Why don't you all just kiss and make up?"

"No, this is what he wanted. He had all the opportunity for it to not go this way. He wanted to end things, so I gave him his wish."

"I can't take this. Have fun attempting to make him jealous!"

Meghan walked off and started a conversation with some nearby acquaintances. Ryse stood alone as she tried to watch Coby out the corner of her eye. Suddenly a handsome man walked up to Ryse and introduced himself, "Hi, don't I know you from somewhere?"

Ryse was startled from her spying on Coby and turned her attention to the handsome gentleman, "No. I'm sorry. I don't think I know you."

"Yes, I know you from somewhere. I never forget a face."

"Well, have you been to one of these parties before? Maybe we've seen each other at a previous function."

"No, I don't think that's it. I don't come to these often, so it has to be from somewhere else."

Ryse balled her mouth up awkwardly and tried to think, "Well, do you live in Southlake Park?"

"Yes, I do. Actually on the north-east side on Earl Street."

"Really? I live right on Maurice Street. Are we neighbors? I frequent the Starbucks over there on Clark and Fosters Road."

The handsome man smiled, "Yes! That is where I know you from. I'm Bobby, and your name is?"

He held out his hand to shake Ryse's, she smiled back and extended her hand to his, "I'm Ryse, nice to meet you."

"*Ryse?* Is it short for something?"

"No. Actually, it's a family name on my mother's side. It was her maiden name. When she got married, she was the last living Ryse of her family, so she passed the name down to me."

"Wow. Great story. Do you plan on passing it down as well?"

"Actually, yes, I do. If I have children, I plan on giving my first born the middle name of Ryse."

"Oh, you have no children?"

"Nope. Unfortunately not yet."

Bobby lean over to look at Ryse's hand, "I see you're not married yet, either."

Ryse lifted up her hand, making the *single ladies* motion, "Nope. Not married yet, either."

"Wow, who is the dummy that let you get away?"

Just as Bobby asked his question, Coby walked up to both of them. Upon Ryse noticing him, she mumbled under her breath, "Speaking of dummies."

"What was that?" Bobby leaned in to hear what Ryse had mumbled.

"No, nothing," she awkwardly said. "I was just mumbling something to myself." Ryse turned toward Coby, "Hi, Mr. St. Williams."

"Really? *Mr. St. Williams?* Is that what we're on now?"

Ryse turned to Bobby, "Bobby? Meet Jacob St. Williams, Jacob meet Bobby."

"Coby. Call me, Coby." Coby reached out to shake Bobby's hand.

"Hi, Coby! Actually, I know exactly who you are. I've followed your career for a while now."

Coby smiled, "No business talk, we're here to celebrate the opening of this fine establishment. How do you know Ryse?"

"Oh, we're neighbors. How do you know, Ryse?"

Before Coby could answer Ryse grabbed Bobby's hand and whisked him away. Coby chuckled to himself and goes back to entertain the guest he brought with him.

Bobby was looking confused, "Did I miss something?"

"No, not at all. That's just an old friend of mine. He knows my ex, and I just felt like he had come over just to spy. I just didn't want to entertain the drama."

"Oh, yeah, I can understand that. So tell me more about yourself." Bobby said as he took a sip of his drink.

"Well, I own an investment firm, K.W. Group. Grew up right here in Southlake Park and love Black art. What about you?"

"Well, I'm a budding sports agent. Worked for a sports management firm for some time as an assistant, and now I'm trying my hand at agency work. My client is the owner of the bar."

"Oh, you're the agent for Kency Thomas?"

"Yes. I helped him get his deal with the Chicago Eagles."

"Oh, wow. Well, you did well for your first client. Congrats!"

Just as they were getting into their conversation Ryse felt her phone vibrating in her bag. She looked down into her purse and retrieved her phone. She unlocked her phone and then looked at the text message from Coby. *Oh, is that your new boyfriend?* Ryse laughed out loud after reading the text.

"Is everything alright?" Bobby asked.

"Yes, absolutely." Ryse's phone vibrated again, she looked down at it. *So, you're going to ignore me?* The text read. "Excuse me, Bobby! Let me take care of something."

Ryse hurried off to the women's bathroom where she happened to bump into Meghan.

"Hey, girl! I saw that fine brother you were talking to. Who is that?" Meghan asked.

"Girl, my neighbor. Well, I just found out he is my neighbor. But wait, let me respond to this fool, Coby."

"What's going on?" Meghan asked.

"One second, I'll tell you in a minute." Ryse quickly began texting on her phone. *You have a whole lot of nerve asking me if he is my boyfriend. You've paraded women all over Southlake Park, and now you're in your feelings 'cause you see me talking to some guy? Get over yourself.* Ryse pressed send.

"Ryse, what's going on?"

"So Coby sees me talking to the guy, he comes over and introduces himself, and now he's texting me asking if he is my boyfriend."

Meghan laughed out loud, "What did you say?"

Ryse handed her the phone and let her read her reply. Meghan laughed again and handed Ryse the phone back.

"I'm convinced he's a narcissist," Ryse said.

"No, he's not. You both are just childish. Both of you all need to surrender to each other and get back together."

"I don't want him anymore."

"Chile, please! Yes, you do. My dead momma can see that all the way from heaven that you want to be with that man."

Ryse pursed her lips, "No, I don't. It's just we keep running into each other at these stupid events. And it's not helping that the press is still asking me questions about Coby. It's like I'm not getting the opportunity to move on because he just keeps reappearing in my life."

"Ryse, you do know that you're not obligated to come to these events? Especially the ones that you know, Coby is going to be at."

"Whose side are you on?" Ryse blabbered.

"Neither one of y'alls. I'm on the side of love." Meghan blew a kiss at Ryse and grabbed her hand and lead her out of the bathroom.

Just as they were entering back into the main entertaining space Ryse spots Coby cuddled up with his date. She felt a tinge of jealously sprout up inside of her. It was her turn to introduce herself.

"Don't you dare," Meghan said as she saw what Ryse was about to do.

"Watch me!"

Ryse began to make her way toward them. As she drew closer, Coby looks up from his female companion and sees Ryse. His smile instantly turns to a frown, as he attempted to move his female companion along.

"Coby!" Ryse yelled out.

Coby's date stops and turns around to see who was calling out his name. She makes eye contact with Ryse and Ryse smiled at her, she didn't smile back.

"Hi, Ryse, good seeing you," Coby says as if it was his first time seeing her all night.

"Hi, Coby, how are you? And who may I ask is your lovely date?"

"I'm Amber!" The woman said sarcastically.

"Hi, Amber, I'm…"

"Ryse. Ryse Taylor. I know who you are."

Ryse clutched her imaginary pearls, "Well, oh my, OK. Well glad to make your acquaintance, Amber. I was just coming over here to say hi to my friend. No harm, no foul."

Ryse then went in and hugged Coby very tightly and then kissed him on the cheek. Then she looked him in the face and kissed him on the lips.

"Ryse?" Coby said, feeling embarrassed.

"Hey, old friend. I just wanted to make sure I said hi before leaving the party."

"Really, Coby?" Amber said, pissed.

Ryse walked away, feeling avenged. Her and Meghan left for the night.

The next morning Ryse woke up to her phone ringing, it was Meghan telling her to look at the messages she had sent her. A local gossip website had done a piece on Ryse and Coby. There were pictures of Ryse, Coby, Bobby, and Amber in the article. The writer named the article, "Who's with Who?"

The sly reporter somehow Photoshopped all of them with each other at different times during the event. Ryse was livid and felt like she was caught in the middle of a scandal.

"Are you kidding me?" Ryse yelled.

"Girl, I know. Isn't it crazy? Has Coby reached out to you?"

Ryse was silent as she checked her phone. "Girl, no. He hasn't. He probably hasn't seen the pictures yet, but I'm sure his phone is going off with notifications."

Ryse blew raspberries, and the light air from her mouth flipped a piece of her bang back. She sat on the edge of the bed, feeling slightly embarrassed.

"Girl, don't worry about all of this. I sure it will blow over and soon be old news."

"I can't believe we carried on like that last night. And poor Bobby got caught up in this mess," Ryse said, shaking her head and putting her hand in her face.

Meghan was chuckling over the phone, "Where do you know him from again?"

"Chile, apparently he's my neighbor. I hope I don't run into him anytime soon at the freaking Starbucks."

Meghan couldn't help herself from hysterically laughing. The entire event was quite amusing to her.

"I'm sure Ms. Amber is enjoying her fifteen minutes of fame."

Meghan said, still laughing, "I'm sure she is. I wonder if she's with Coby right now. They were quite boo'd up last night."

"Meghan!" Ryse yelled, irritated.

"What?"

"This is not funny!" Ryse was about to blow a gasket, "*I wonder if she's with Coby right now?*" She said mimicking Meghan. "He better not be!"

"Oh, really? I thought you didn't want him anymore?"

"I don't."

Meghan scoffed, "So why do you care if he's with Amber or not?"

"Bye, Meghan!" Ryse hung up the phone.

Ryse lifted herself from the bed and went to her bathroom to get the rest of her day going. As she brushed her teeth and washed her face, she couldn't help but think about Coby.

The Submission

"Do you take this woman to be your lawfully wedded wife?" The pastor said, staring at the blushing groom.

"I do," he said with great glee.

Then the middle-aged pastor looked at the tearful bride, "Do you take this man to be your lawfully wedded husband?"

A single tear fell down the bride's face, and she squeezed his hands really tightly, "I do!" She said with a mouthful cry.

The bride began to bounce up and down as she anticipated the next words to come out of the pastor's mouth, joining her with her handsome groom together.

"Well, let me get this moving before the bride beat me to the punch," the pastor said jokingly. A sea of laughter went throughout the audience. "With the powers vested in me, I now pronounce you man and wife. You may now kiss your bride!"

The bride grabbed the groom's face, and sensually kissed him as if it was the first time she ever placed her lips on him. The audience began to clap and whistle at the intimacy shared between the couple. After they finished their minute-long kiss, they finally came up for air and turned toward the crowd blushing.

"I now present to you, Mr. and Mrs. Reginald James!" The pastor gleefully announced as the couple began to walk down the aisle during the procession of the wedding ceremony.

"That was beautiful," Ryse said as she watched the couple come past her row that she sat in next to Coby.

"Yes, it was," he responded.

Ryse quickly got up and walked away from Coby and went to mingle with the other guests of the wedding. Coby and Ryse had been invited to Coby's close friend's wedding four months before their split. Ryse had become quite familiar with the groom's fiancée, and they kept in touch, even after Coby and she had broken up. The bride insisted on Ryse coming to the wedding and reception.

Ryse was hesitant to appear at the wedding to avoid rumors swarming that they were back together, but the bride assured Ryse that the wedding would be private and no media would be present. After Ryse and Coby's last interaction at the bar opening, Ryse made it her business to not go to any more functions that Coby would be at.

They hadn't seen each other in months, nor had they spoken to each other. Coby had sent a few text messages every once in a while to see how she was doing, but nothing more than hi and bye.

Coby started to mingle around to the cocktail area where the guests were held until the reception was ready to start. He stayed close to the bar while watching Ryse as she moved around the room. He wanted to talk to her, but he realized Ryse had made it clear that she wasn't trying to be near him.

Suddenly Coby felt a tap on his shoulder and turned around quickly. He smiled, it was an old friend name Thomas, whom he hadn't see in a while.

"My man, how have you been?" Thomas said.

"Thomas, wow! It's been about two years, huh? How's LA treating you?"

"Well. Treating me well! Who would have thought a vegan restaurant would go so well?"

"I told you," Coby said as he pointed to him in an I-told-you-so-way.

"Yeah, that was the best advice you could have given me. LA folks love some vegan food."

"You thinking about another location? Maybe here in Southlake Park?"

"I have a few locations in mind, but I'm working the numbers to see how that will work out."

"Yeah, I hear you." Coby stopped and lost his train of thought as Ryse comes into view and walks past him. His eyes followed her, and Thomas noticed.

"Hey, man. What's going on with that? Who is that?" Thomas inquired.

"Aww, man, that's my ex." Coby sighed.

"What happened? Is it drama?"

"No, drama. Just something I messed up."

"How?" Thomas asked as he looked at Ryse again and scratched his head.

"I let my ego get in the way and didn't tell her how I was feeling completely."

Thomas let out a hearty laugh, "Oh, she's the one who got away, huh?"

"I guess you can say that."

"Well, you two are here, so why don't you make a move?"

"Naw, that's over. I can't even say that we're friends."

Just as Thomas was going to respond, a woman walks up to him and kisses him on the cheek. Coby recognizes her right away, it's Thomas' wife.

"Coby! How are you? Long time no see!"

Coby leaned in to hug her, "Yes, good seeing you, Lorraine! I was just talking to Thomas about you all's vegan restaurant."

"Yes, it's going great! Life is great!" Lorraine turned to Thomas, "Hey, babe. I want you to meet someone." Then Lorraine turned to Coby, "I'm sorry, can I steal him away?"

Coby slightly bows his head, "Of course, no problem. It was really nice running into you all!"

They hugged Coby and walked off. Coby was back standing alone as he searched the room again to see if he could find Ryse. For a full five minutes, he looked around the room but couldn't see her anywhere. He then pulled out his phone from his pocket and checked his email quickly, and then goes back to looking for Ryse again, still no sign of her. He assumed she had left and went on to mingle throughout the room.

As another thirty minutes passed, the wedding coordinator announced that the reception room was open and that guests should stop at the hostess table to get their table seating. Coby walks up to the table after having two new drinks at the bar. He wasn't sure why he was still at the wedding, but he had blocked the entire day off, so he figured he may as well enjoy his day.

"Your name, sir?" The hostess assistant asked as Coby walked up to the table.

"Jacob St. Williams."

The hostess assistant looked down at her list, searching for Coby's name. As her pen moved up and down the paper, she finally stopped and looked back up, "Mr. St. Williams, you'll be seated at table six. It's within that first row of tables in front of the head table."

"Thank you," he said as he took a small card that she gave to him and then he walked into the reception room.

The room was grand! All white porcelain columns and marble ceilings. Crystal chandeliers and the wedding colors of coral and violet sprinkled throughout the room. Coby searched the room and started walking toward the front tables. He quickly glanced at the numbers until he saw table six.

There were place settings on the table, and he spotted his name right away. He sat down in front of his table and looked around at all the other guests who were coming into the room.

While he wasn't paying attention, he felt a presence come up behind him. He turned around, and his face light up.

"Hi, Coby."

Coby smiled and stood up, helping Ryse into her seat next to him, "Hey, Ryse. I thought you left?" Coby then sat back down in his chair and then looked at the place setting. He wanted to make sure that Ryse indeed should have been sitting next to him.

"No, I didn't leave. I went outside to clear my head. It was too loud for me in the cocktail area. Plus the scenery is beautiful. I bet it's even more elaborate at night."

"Yeah, I bet. So how have you been?"

Ryse smiled, "I've been OK. How about you?"

"I've been good."

An awkward silence fell upon them, and they just stared at each other for a bit, and then they both started looking around the room.

Coby turned back to Ryse, and just as he started to open his mouth, a woman's voice came over the loudspeaker.

"Ladies and gentlemen, may I have your attention. Please join me as I introduce the bridal party of the James' wedding!"

The crowd began to cheer and clap. Ryse and Coby directed their attention to the woman dressed in a formal coral dress with a beautiful, soft up-do. Loud, energetic music began to play, and everyone started dancing in their seats. The wedding coordinator started naming groomsmen and bridesmaids off one by one.

"Now ladies and gents, please rise to your feet as we introduce Mr. and Mrs. Reginald James!"

The same energetic music played even louder, and everyone stood to their feet clapping, cheering, and smiling as the lovely couple comes in. The couple stopped in the middle of the reception dance floor and does a dance as everyone looked upon. After two more dances, they make their way around the room, greeting their guests and mingling.

By now, the table that Coby and Ryse are occupying is full of the other guests assigned to the table. They don't say much to each other and make small talk with the other guests. The usual wedding activities occur. The waiters and waitresses delivered the food to the tables, and the guests eat. Different guests rose up to give their well wishes, and the wedding party said their speeches.

The inevitable tossing of the bouquet comes around. The wedding coordinator retakes the microphone. "OK, where are all my single ladies?!" She roared.

All the single women began to stand up and walk to the center of the dance floor. Ryse stayed in her seat.

Coby noticed that she didn't get up. Concern washed over his face, "Oh, you're not single anymore?" He said to Ryse.

Ryse laughed, "Of course I am. I just don't want to do this stupid bouquet thing."

Coby nudged her, jokingly, "Go, head. You know you want to."

"No, I really don't. "

"Girl, get up there and play nice. It's just fun."

"OK, bet. When they do the men, you better get your single tail up there."

Coby winked at her and Ryse got up to join the women waiting patiently for the bride to toss the bouquet.

Of course, the bride did the traditional two fake outs before she actually threw the bouquet. As the bouquet went flying in the air, Ryse watched as it arched over and fell nowhere near her direction. She laughed as the women pushed each other out of the way to be the lucky once catching the bouquet. Some lady who came in an ill-fitting green dress and hooker heels was the lucky recipient.

Soon it was Coby's turn to stand to catch the ceremonial garter. He stood right in the center as if he wanted to make sure he had a chance of catching the garter, should it come his way. As the groom teased his bride and fondled her under her dress, he soon revealed the garter and didn't waste any time throwing it at the men that were standing near.

The garter made its direction toward Coby, he extended his arms to make a reasonable effort to catch it.

But he was out jumped by the guy standing next to him. Coby laughed it off and then went back to his seat sitting next to Ryse.

"Wow, it looked like you were really attempting to catch that garter."

"Well, I was trying to be a good sport!" Coby said as beads of perspiration formed on his forehead.

Ryse noticed it too, "Here, let me wipe your head." She grabbed the napkin from the table and wiped his forehead. Coby smiled.

Just as he was about to open his mouth, he was interrupted once again by someone speaking on the microphone, this time it was the bride.

"Ladies and gentlemen, I just want to personally thank you for coming and sharing this special day with us. We will cherish this moment for the rest of our lives."

The crowd ooh'd and aww'd at the blushing bride. Just as she was speaking the wait staff came around to bring dessert and after dinner coffee and tea to the guests.

The bride continued to speak, "During the reception check-in, some of you were randomly selected and given cards. If you were one of those random people, please stand to your feet."

The entire room began to look around to see who were the randomly selected people, to both of their surprises, Coby and Ryse both had cards in their hands.

The bride continued, "Now, you six people will open these cards and speak the words of wisdom that I want everyone to listen closely to. Not only are you speaking wisdom to myself and Reginald, but speaking wisdom to all those in the room currently in love, looking for love, and married."

The wedding coordinator starts to walk around the room to each individual person that has a card. She gets to the first person, a very tall and handsome gentleman and hands him the microphone so he can speak what's on his card.

"Love is about give and take. Always find the balance," he said as the crowd melts.

The coordinator walks over to the next person, this time a much older grey-haired man. "When you get into an argument, listen to what the other person is trying to say through the anger. Anger is a surface emotion. There is more to it than meets the eye."

The crowd clapped and shook their head as they were in agreement with what he read off the card. The coordinator then goes to the next person, the previous guest's wife, who was seated next to him.

"Your marriage is not made up of only two people. God should always be there. He will always be the referee." She read.

"Now, I like that," the coordinator said as she quickly made her way across the room to a sexy woman in blue who stood with her card in her hand. "Lady in blue, what does your card say?"

"Nobody wins when the family feuds."

All of the guests under forty years of age started laughing as they are familiar with the rapper, Jay Z line from one of his most recent songs.

Finally, the coordinator makes her way to Coby and Ryse. She hands the microphone to Ryse first and let her read what was on her card.

"There can't be two alphas at home. Someone needs to be the alpha, and someone needs to be the beta," Ryse read and then looked at Coby.

Coby grabbed the microphone from Ryse and then looked down at his card, "Submission is required of both parties if love is going to be enduring."

"Wow!" Ryse mumbled to herself as she takes in all the words that are spoken from the cards.

The coordinator goes on to say closing remarks before they allow the guests and wedding party to go back to enjoying the rest of the evening. Coby and Ryse watched everyone as they laughed and enjoyed the open bar and good dancing.

Coby finally turned to Ryse, "You look beautiful today."

Ryse smiled, "Thank you. You're very handsome as well."

"I miss you."

Ryse looked at Coby and didn't say a word. She looked out over the reception room, then turned to look out of the window and noticed that the sun had set and the outside lights had lit up the patio and pond area. She turned back to Coby, "It's noisy in here. Let's go outside and enjoy the scenery."

Ryse grabbed Coby's hand and gently tugged on him to get out of his seat. Ryse started to lead the way out of the reception room, holding Coby's hand, but Coby stopped and pulled her back.

Ryse looked at Coby puzzled, "What's wrong?"

Coby pulled Ryse closed to him and said, "No, I'm the alpha!" And lead them out of the reception room onto the patio.

About the Author

Ty Young is a mother, author, blogger, graphic creator, and budding filmmaker. She embraces all of her gifts and uses them equally as an expression of her passions.

To date, she has published five books, _My Journey to Life_, _The Uncertain Journey of Love & Marriage_, _Purple Potpourri & Sacred Vulnerability_, _The Black Girl Book_, and _The Alpha Bid: Distinguished Gentleman Series._ Be on the lookout for four more title debuting soon, _When Lust Has Conceived, The Rules of Engagement, The King and his Wives,_ and _Delusions of Grandeur._

You can also find her blogging at Circapuprle, where she writes about her faith, soul, and opinion in an in your face type of way. She likes to declare that she's not holy enough for the church, but not worldly enough for the world. Ty likes to have conversations that we're afraid to talk about, but desperately need to talk about within the church and the world. She writes in the color of *purple*, purple is her aura, it's her personality, it's her thing.

Ty also is a prolific graphic designer, releasing her artistic passions through her graphic design company, Young Dreams Media.

And lastly, she has been pursuing her dream of becoming a filmmaker. Ty is currently working on a 40-minute short documentary entitled, *Saturday Flowers*, aka #PURPLESFILMPROJECT. Right now she is in the crowdfunding and production phase of the project. If you would like to donate, learn more at www.circapurple.com/purplesfilmproject.